SING, HENRIETTA! SING!

By **Lynn Downey**

Illustrated by
Tony Sansevero

Ideals Children's Books • Nashville, Tennessee
an imprint of Hambleton-Hill Publishing, Inc.

To Skip and the Beans.
—L. D.

To my insane vegetarian friends.
And special thanks to you, Gene.
—T. S.

Text copyright © 1997 by Lynn Downey
Illustrations copyright © 1997 by Hambleton-Hill Publishing, Inc.

Published by Ideals Children's Books
An imprint of Hambleton-Hill Publishing, Inc.
Nashville, Tennessee 37218

Printed and bound in Mexico

Library of Congress Cataloging-in-Publication Data
Downey, Lynn, 1961–
      Sing, Henrietta! Sing! / by Lynn Downey ; illustrated by Tony
Sansevero.
         p.   cm.
      Summary: Customers are eager to buy Henrietta and George's
beautiful vegetables, but are frightened away by Henrietta's
terrible singing. Then Henrietta and George find out the plants
thrive only when Henrietta sings.
      ISBN 1-57102-103-5
      [I. Vegetable gardening—Fiction. 2. Gardening—Fiction.
3. Singing—Fiction.] I. Sansevero, Tony, ill. II. Title.
PZ7.D75915Si   1997
[Fic]—dc20   96-38638
                                  CIP
                                   AC

The illustrations in this book were rendered in watercolor gouache and colored pencil.
The type was set in Dominican.
Color separations were made by Color 4, Inc.
Printed and bound by R.R. Donnelley & Sons Company.

First Edition

10 9 8 7 6 5 4 3 2 1

Henrietta and George had been neighbors for **23** years.
What's more, they were the best of friends.

Each spring, on a small patch of grass between their houses, Henrietta and George planted a lovely vegetable garden.

Henrietta loved to sing in the garden. She sang while she planted. "AhhhUUUGA!" She sang while she weeded. "EeeeeeeYaaaaaaa!" She even sang while she picked. "UuuuuuuEEEEEAAAEE!"

The problem was that whenever Henrietta sang chipmunks scrambled for their holes, robins' eggs trembled in their nests, and geese flying north quickly turned south again.

"My Daddy always said, 'Plants like a good song,'" Henrietta had explained to George long ago. "'The louder, the better,' he'd say."

And George, being a kind man, never had the heart to tell Henrietta how badly she sang. So he learned to just smile and whistle along and, after a few years, he almost got used to it.

Besides, despite Henrietta's singing, the garden *did* grow beautifully. Not only did their vegetables win first place at the state fair every summer, but everyone wanted to buy some.

Year after year, the orders poured in. Their garden grew bigger and bigger until, after 23 years, Henrietta and George could barely keep up with the deliveries *and* the tending.

"What we need is a farm," Henrietta joked one day.

"Henrietta!" George exclaimed. "You're a genius! Next spring we can use both our yards—every inch—just like a farm and set out a stand by the road! No more orders. No more deliveries. Why—we may even become rich!"

And so, all winter long, Henrietta and George drew up plans for their new garden.

On the sign:

WHERE YA GOING?
FRESH vegetables
THAT WAY!

On the crate: VEGETABLES

On the house: FEED

At first thaw, George began tilling until not one blade of grass was left standing.

By summer, the garden was ready. They sent out flyers and posted signs along the road. When the big day finally arrived, Henrietta worked in the garden while George waited at their roadside stand.

Old Joe Hubert, the baker from town, was George's first customer. "Howdy, George," Old Joe said. "How about selling me a dozen or so of those delicious..." "EEEYAAAAA!" Henrietta's earsplitting melody rose from the garden.

Joe's eyes grew as big as golf balls.

"UUUUUUEEEEEEE!" Henrietta continued to sing. Terrified, Old Joe jumped
in his car and sped off. And that was just the beginning.

All day long, cars whizzed by, frantically rolling up their windows as they passed. Two officers from the National Park Service did stop though. They were investigating reports of a wounded buffalo in the area. When George explained that it was only Henrietta singing, the officers apologized and quickly left.

George tried everything he could think of to improve business. He moved the stand farther up the road, but he could still hear Henrietta singing. He even lowered the prices, but with Henrietta shrieking in the background, no one wanted to stop.

Sadly, George had no other choice but to tell Henrietta the truth. She was silent for a long time.

"Is it that bad?" Henrietta finally asked.

George nodded.

"Well, then," said Henrietta, "there's only one thing to do. Tomorrow I'll stop singing. Forever."

The next day George sold 36 dozen ears of corn, 85 tomatoes, and 152 cucumbers. He could hardly wait to share the good news with Henrietta.

"I'm happy, George. Really," she said, trying to smile. But Henrietta didn't look happy at all. She looked tired.

By the week's end, George sold every last vegetable they had harvested so far. But for some reason, the garden began looking as tired as Henrietta. The tomatoes stayed green, the corn drooped, and the cucumbers were squishy.

They tried everything they could to make the garden grow as it had before. More water . . . less water . . . more fertilizer . . . less fertilizer. Nothing worked. The garden, it seemed, was dying. Finally, George put out a *Closed* sign on the stand.

That evening, George sat in the moonlight, staring at the garden and feeling pretty tired himself. Henrietta swung on her porch swing. She was watching the sky and one star in particular as it twinkled and glittered. Very quietly, and without thinking at all, Henrietta began to sing,

"*Twinkle, twinkle, little star. How I wonder what you are . . . .*"

Suddenly George noticed a tomato plant quiver. He rubbed his eyes and looked again. Corn stalks began to stiffen and stand upright, as though straining to hear Henrietta sing.

Amazed, George cried, "Henrietta!"

"Sorry, George," Henrietta sighed. "I forgot."

"No," George said. "Don't stop. Sing, Henrietta! Sing!"

Henrietta ran over and joined George in the garden.

"Sing, Henrietta! Sing!" he cried again. "They love you!"

Henrietta sang quietly at first. But as the entire garden leaned toward her, she sang louder . . . and Louder . . . and LOUDER—until she reached a full-blown Henrietta screech!

The whole garden rocked back and forth in time with Henrietta's song. Henrietta's terrible voice was amazing! The louder she shrieked, the more the garden swayed, until at last when she stopped—sometime long into the night—the whole garden rustled as if a wind had suddenly passed through. It sounded almost like . . . clapping.

FRESH
VEGETABLES
SOLD
HERE!

Best this side
OF THE
Mississippi!

FREE EARPLUGS with
EVERY PURCHASE!

Within a week, George had reopened the stand. Not only was the garden booming with beautiful vegetables and Henrietta's voice once again, but business was booming too. Of course the new signs George put up helped quite a bit!

That summer, George and Henrietta made enough money to buy
a little farm just outside of town. They called it Music to Our Ears.
They weren't rich, but they were happy—and what's more,
they stayed the best of friends.

DATE DUE		
MAR 1 1 1998		
MAR 27 1998		
APR 16 1998		
SEP 25 1998		
OCT 19 1998		
NOV 9 1998		
DEC 7		
OCT 20 2003		

F
DOW

Downey, Lynn.

Sing, Henrietta!
Sing!